GREAT BLACK HEROES

FIVE NOTABLE INVENTORS

by Wade Hudson
Illustrated by Ron Garnett

Hello Reader! – Level 4

Scholastic Inc.

Cartwheel ·B·O·O·K·S· ®

New York Toronto London Auckland Sydney

Produced by Just Us Books, Inc.

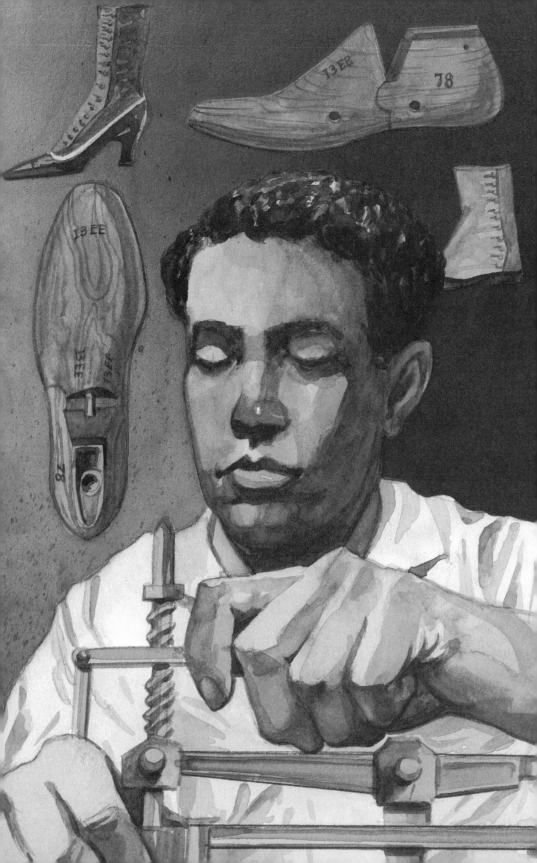

Jan Ernst Matzeliger

"He Made Shoes to Last"
born 1852 — died 1889

There once was a time when most people could not buy shoes. Shoes were expensive because it took a long time to make each pair.

Jan Ernst Matzeliger changed that. He invented a machine that made shoes quickly and cheaply.

Jan was born September 15, 1852, in South America. His father was white and his mother was black. When he was a boy, Jan worked in his father's shop. In the shop,

workers made metal tools, ornaments, and containers. Jan learned how to use the lathe machine that cut and shaped the metal.

During his free time, he would go down to the river and watch the ships. He would dream about sailing out to sea.

At the age of 19, Jan became a seaman. He sailed on a ship to the Far East. Two years later, in 1873, the ship landed in the United States in the city of Philadelphia. There, Jan tried to find a job as a machine operator. But every machine shop he went to turned him away. Slavery had ended ten years before Jan arrived in the United States. But many whites still did not respect blacks. They did not want to hire blacks for factory jobs. Jan was sad but he kept looking. Finally, he was hired by a shoemaker.

Jan learned to operate the McKay machine. It sewed leather together to make the soles of shoes. Jan was good at operating this machine. He wanted to learn more about shoe-making.

In 1877, Jan moved to Lynn, Massachusetts. The city was called the "shoe industry capital of the world." Most of the people there worked for shoe companies. After days of looking for a job, Jan was hired at the Harney Brothers factory.

Jan liked all the different machines. Some cut and sewed the upper parts of the shoes. Some attached the upper parts of the shoes to the soles. Others made buttonholes.

It was difficult for Jan to find work in Lynn, Massachusetts.

The hardest part of shoe-making was connecting the upper part to the innersole. This step is called *lasting*. It had to be done by hand. The leather had to be stretched over a wooden model of a foot called a *last*. Then the finished shape had to be tacked into place onto the sole. There was no machine to do this important work.

Jan decided he was going to invent such a machine. People laughed when they heard Jan was trying to make a machine that could last shoes. Other workers had tried and failed. No one can make that kind of machine, they thought. They made awful jokes about Jan.

By the fall of 1880, Jan had made a model of his machine from cigar boxes. He was sure that once his model was made into a real machine, it would work. Another inventor who was working on the same idea offered Jan $50.00 for it. Fifty dollars was a lot of money in those days and Jan was very poor. But he said no.

Jan needed to use a forge and a lathe machine to make his invention from metal. A

Jan invented his machine at the West Lynn Mission. He rented a room there from a black family named Taylor.

Other workers laughed when they heard Jan was trying to make a machine to last shoes.

forge is a furnace where metal is heated. Then the metal is hammered and bent into shape on the lathe machine. The Harney Brothers didn't have either machine. So Jan went to work for the Beal Company. This company let him use their forge and lathe.

By 1882, Jan had made a model out of scrap metal. It lasted shoes perfectly. Jan had done what others had said was impossible. Jan knew, however, that this machine made from scrap metal could not work for long before falling apart. He would have to make a machine with new metal parts. Once again, another inventor offered to buy Jan's invention. This time Jan was offered $1,500.00. Again he said no.

Two businessmen gave Jan the money he needed to make his new machine. In return, they would receive two-thirds of any money that Jan might make. The three men formed the Union Lasting Machine Company.

On March 20, 1883, Jan was given a patent from the United States government for his new lasting machine. The patent is a special certificate. It gives the inventor the right to be the only one to make and sell an important invention.

Jan's invention could last from 300 to 700 pairs of shoes in a ten-hour workday. One person doing the same work by hand could only finish 50 pairs of shoes in that time. Soon, many shoe companies wanted Jan's invention.

Jan and his business partners didn't have enough money to fill the large number of orders for the lasting machine. New business partners took over Jan's company. They formed a bigger company called the Consolidated Lasting Machine Company. Jan was given a share of the company.

In the years that followed, Jan's invention made many other people very rich. But he was almost forgotten.

Jan shakes hands with one of the men who gave money to help build his shoe-lasting machine.

Jan sent this diagram of his invention to the United States Patent Office.

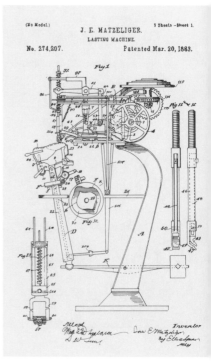

These men worked in a shoe factory using Jan's invention.

Jan Matzeliger's shoe-lasting machine.

Jan had gone without food in order to save money to build his machine. He had worked long hours. His health was not good. On August 24, 1889, Jan died. He was only 36 years old. His great invention had changed the shoe industry and made shoes available to all people.

In 1992, the United States government printed a special postage stamp to honor this great inventor.

Fig 1

C

c

H

Fig 2

Elijah McCoy.

Elijah McCoy

"The Real McCoy"
born 1843 — died 1929

Young Elijah McCoy loved machines. He would take things apart just to see how they worked. Then he would put the parts back together again. People knew Elijah was very smart. And they knew he would do something very special when he grew up.

Elijah was born in Colchester, Ontario, Canada. His parents had escaped there from slavery in the United States. The McCoys made sure their children went to school. They wanted them to have a good education.

When Elijah was 16 years old, he went to school in Scotland to learn drafting. Drafters draw plans for new machines and buildings. Workers use the drawings to build the machines or buildings. Elijah also studied engineering. Engineers plan how to build such things as canals, bridges, and oil wells.

Elijah studied hard. He finished his training and became a "master mechanic and engineer."

Elijah studied hard while attending school in Scotland.

Elijah decided to live in Ypsilanti, Michigan. But he could not find a job as an engineer. Although slavery had ended in the United States, there still was prejudice against black people. Elijah had to accept a job as a fireman and oilman for the Michigan Central Railroad.

Elijah had to shovel tons of coal into the firebox of the train. It was hard work.

At that time, trains ran on steam. Steam was made when water was heated in boilers by burning coal.

Elijah had other work, too. He oiled moving parts of the train. Every few miles the train would stop so that Elijah could oil the parts.

If parts rubbed together, they could stick and stop the train. Oil kept the parts from sticking. Oiling moving parts of a train or machine is called lubricating.

Elijah wanted to find a better way to lubricate the moving parts. Other people had

Moving parts on trains had to be oiled often.

tried to make oiling tools. But none of them worked very well. Elijah thought about it and came up with an answer.

In 1872, Elijah made his first oil cup. This invention dripped oil to the parts that needed lubricating. Later that year, the United States government gave Elijah a patent to protect the rights to his invention.

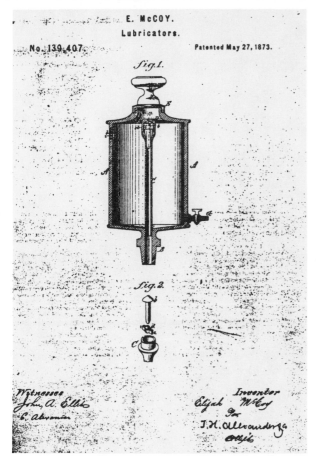

Elijah McCoy's automatic lubricator.

Elijah called his new invention the "lubricating cup."

Railroad executives didn't trust Elijah's invention at first. They didn't think that a black man could be smart enough to invent such an important tool. But they were wrong.

Finally, the Michigan Central Railroad gave the new invention a try. It worked

Elijah worked very hard to make his invention better.

perfectly. The news of McCoy's "lubricating cup" spread quickly. Soon, all of the railroad companies wanted to use Elijah's invention.

Others tried to copy Elijah's lubricating cup. None worked as well as Elijah's. And companies knew the difference. They would always ask for "the real McCoy." Today, that expression is still used to mean the "real thing."

In 1882, Elijah began to work full time as an inventor. He invented an ironing board and a lawn sprinkler. But most of his inventions were for oiling different kinds of machines. In all, Elijah received 57 patents for inventions.

In 1920, Elijah McCoy formed his own business in Detroit, Michigan. It was called the Elijah McCoy Manufacturing Company. He operated it until a year before his death. By 1928, Elijah was in bad health. He had used all the money he earned on improving his inventions. Elijah entered a home for the poor and elderly. A year later, he died.

In 1975, this talented inventor was honored by the city of Detroit. A historic marker was placed at the site of his home. A street was also named in his honor.

Granville T. Woods

"The Greatest Electrician in the World"
born 1856 — died 1910

When people called Granville T. Woods "the Black Edison" it was meant to be an honor. They were comparing him to Thomas Alva Edison, who was known as one of the greatest inventors who ever lived. Granville Woods made many important inventions, too.

Granville T. Woods was born April 23, 1856. He left school when he was ten years old and worked in a machine shop. After that, he had many different jobs. He was a fireman with a railroad company in Missouri. It was his job to shovel coal into the firebox of the train. He worked in a steel mill in Springfield, Ohio.

In New York City, Granville found a job in a machine shop. He went to school at night to learn about electricity.

When Granville was 22 years old, he worked on a British steamship called *Ironsides*. For two years, he visited many parts of the world. Then he returned to the United States and settled in Cincinnati, Ohio.

In 1884, Granville T. Woods began his career as one of America's most talented inventors. His first invention helped steam boiler furnaces heat homes and buildings better. Later that year, Granville invented a new telephone transmitter. It could send sounds over a longer distance than the old transmitters. The sounds were much clearer and louder, too.

Granville loved learning new things.

Granville kept working. In 1885, he invented a wonderful new thing. With Granville's new invention, a person could send a message by *speaking* near telegraph keys. The person on the other end could hear the message just like from a telephone. The American Bell Telephone Company bought the patent from Granville.

Then there was the "amusement apparatus." This was a special set of tracks for motor cars to run on. Because of Granville's new invention, many new rides were set up at amusement parks.

Granville invented an incubator, too. An incubator is a box that helps to keep eggs warm enough to hatch. Today, some incubators can hatch as many as 100,000 baby chicks at once.

One of Granville's most important inventions was railway telegraphy. Engineers and conductors on moving trains used it to talk to one another. Station operators could also talk to operators on moving trains. They could tell each other if there was a problem on the train. And they could stop accidents from happening.

In 1888, Granville invented an overhead electric system to run trains. A pole from the train was attached to an electric line running overhead. The electric line gave the power to make the trains go. Many cities replaced the "old" steam-engine trains with trains operated by Granville's new system.

Another of Granville's important inventions was a safety device called the "third rail." The "third rail" runs alongside of the two tracks on which a train runs. The

Railway "telephony" and telegraphy were two of Granville's most important inventions.

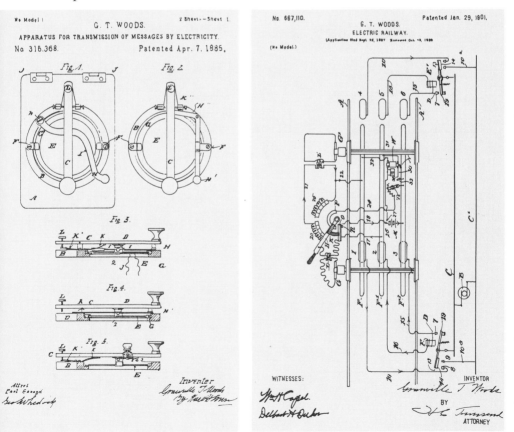

Drawings of two of Granville's inventions.

27

"third rail" provides the power to make the train go. The "third rail" is still used today to help run subway trains in New York City and many other cities.

By 1890, Granville Woods had received 22 patents for his inventions. But Granville had to face many difficulties during his career. He went to court twice to protect his right to the railway telegraph system he invented.

Thomas Edison had been working on a similar system. The Edison Company said Edison had invented the railway telegraph system first. Granville proved he was the original inventor. But he had to spend almost all of his money to do it.

Thomas Edison offered Granville a job with his company. But Granville did not accept. He wanted to be his own boss.

Very few have done more in the field of electricity and railway safety than Granville T. Woods. Yet most people do not know his

Modern trolleys in Boston and San Francisco use Granville's overhead electric system instead of steam-run engines.

A drawing of the overhead conducting system for electric railways.

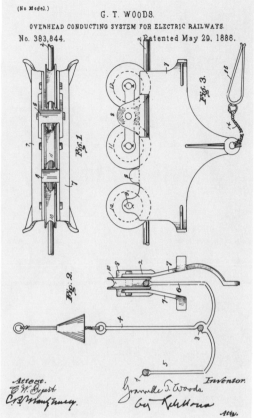

name. Many of Granville's patents were sold to large companies such as General Electric, Westinghouse, and American Bell Telephone.

Granville T. Woods died in 1910. In 1969, a school in Brooklyn, New York, was named for this great inventor. On October 11, 1974, the governor of Ohio issued a proclamation to recognize Granville T. Woods as the "greatest electrician in the world."

Madam C. J. Walker

"A Millionaire Inventor"
born 1867 — died 1919

A common problem helped to start Madam C. J. Walker's career as an inventor and businesswoman. Her hair had begun to fall out. So she invented her own hair grower to stop it. She invented other hair care products, too. She set up her own company to make and sell the products. During the time she lived, this smart woman became the richest black woman in the United States.

Madam C. J. Walker's birth name was Sarah Breedlove. She was born December 23,

1867. Her mother and father worked on a large plantation in Delta, Louisiana.

Sarah and her family lived in a dirt-floor shack on the plantation. There were no doors or windows. There was no water. There was no toilet.

Day after day, Sarah and her family worked in the cotton fields owned by the Burney family. They hoed grass from around the cotton plants. When the cotton was ready for harvest, they picked the boll from the plant. Workers had to bend to reach the plant. They often stayed in a bent position for hours.

When Sarah was seven years old, her mother and father died from yellow fever. Sarah, along with her brother, Alex, and sister, Louvenia, tried to work the land. But they could not do it. Alex moved to Vicksburg, Mississippi, to find other work. Later, when Sarah was ten, she and Louvenia moved there, too.

Madam Walker had to pick cotton as a child.

In 1882, 14-year-old Sarah married Moses McWilliams. In 1885, the couple had a daughter they named A'Lelia. Two years later, Sarah's husband was killed. She was only 20 years old.

Sarah and her daughter moved to St. Louis, Missouri. There she worked as a cook and laundress. During this difficult time, Sarah's hair began to fall out. Nothing she tried would stop it. So she invented her own cure. She made a mixture using ingredients that came to her in a dream.

Sarah was surprised at how quickly her hair grew back. The mixture worked for her friends, too. So Sarah decided to start her own hair care business.

In 1905, Sarah moved to Denver, Colorado. She had very little money saved. But she used it to buy things she needed to start her business. She and her relatives worked in the attic of their home. There they filled many jars with her mixture.

These products were made by Madam Walker.

Some months later, Sarah married a newspaper man named C. J. Walker. She changed her name to Madam C. J. Walker and she called her mixture Madam C. J. Walker's Hair Grower.

Madam Walker couldn't read or write well until later in her life. But she was an excellent businesswoman. She sold her products by going door-to-door and giving free demonstrations. As the businesss grew,

Women who worked for Madam Walker sold her products door-to-door.

she created more products. She began to sell the products by mail. She set up her own factories and laboratories to make the products. She opened beauty parlors in cities in the United States, the Caribbean, and in South America. She also established training schools for the people who worked for her.

In 1910, Madam Walker moved her company to Indianapolis, Indiana. The company continued to grow. By 1919, she had 25,000 women working for the company. The Madam C. J. Walker Manufacturing Company had become the most successful company owned by an African-American woman. Madam C. J. Walker became the first black female millionaire.

Getting a hair treatment with Madam's product.

*These women and men worked for Madam C. J. Walker's company.
They met at national conferences every year.*

*The cabin where Madam
Walker was born.*

*Madam Walker built this
mansion in New York
State.*

Madam C. J. Walker always found time to help her people. She donated money to many black organizations and black schools. She gave to the needy.

"My object in life," she once said, "is not simply to make money for myself or to spend it on myself. I love to use a part of what I make in trying to help others."

Madam Walker and her daugher, A'Lelia, ride in style.

Garrett A. Morgan

"A Champion of Public Safety"
born 1877 — died 1963

On July 24, 1916, there was an explosion in Tunnel Number Five of the Cleveland, Ohio, Water Works. The tunnel lay more than 250 feet below Lake Erie. Thirty-two men were trapped inside the tunnel. Rescuers could not get to the men because the tunnel was filled with dangerous smoke and natural gas.

Garrett Morgan and his brother Frank rushed to the site. They put funny-looking masks over their heads. Garrett had made the

Garrett pulls a worker from the smoke-filled tunnel.

masks. The masks had long tubes with holes at the end. The long tubes were very important. Smoke, dust, and gas rise, leaving cleaner air closer to the ground. The long tubes could reach the cleaner air.

The two brothers entered the tunnel along with two other men. The masks protected the men. They brought out the other men who were trapped inside the tunnel. But not all of the trapped men had survived.

Newspapers all over the country carried the story of Garrett's and Frank's courage. Garrett got a medal for his bravery.

Garrett had made his mask in 1912. The United States government gave Garrett a patent for his invention in 1914. That same year, at a safety and sanitation fair in New York City, Garrett received a gold medal as first prize for his invention. Soon after that, fire departments in some cities began using it. A company was formed to make Garrett's new mask.

Garrett called his invention the "gas inhalator." It sold slowly until the big rescue on July 24, 1916.

Then, people from everywhere wanted to see the funny-looking masks that would let someone walk safely into a smoke-filled tunnel. Fire departments and mining companies were very interested.

In later years, the United States government made some changes to the "gas inhalator." It was then called the gas mask. American soldiers used gas masks during World War I to protect themselves from poisonous gas. They saved many lives.

Garrett Morgan was born in Paris, Kentucky. He had ten brothers and sisters. At the age of 14, Garrett moved to Cincinnati, Ohio, where he worked as a handyman. Later, he moved to Cleveland, Ohio. He started a business there.

Garrett Morgan had only an elementary school education. But he was very smart. He liked to invent things.

His first discovery was a chemical to straighten hair. The G. A. Morgan Hair Cream is believed to be the first human hair straightener.

In 1923, Garrett received a patent for a very important invention. Before 1923, there were no traffic lights. Cars and horse-drawn carriages drove through street intersections at their own risk. There were many crashes.

Morgan's National Safety Hood

Style Two Helmet

Combination Smoke, Gas, Ammonia and Sand Blast Protector.

Garrett A. Morgan published a book showing how to use his national safety hood.

THE NAT·SAFETY·DEVICE·Co
AWARDED·FIRST·GRAND·PRIZE
GOLDEN MEDAL
AT THE

SECOND
INTERNATIONAL
EXPOSITION
OF
SAFETY
AND
SANITATION
NEW YORK CITY
1914
COMMEMORATIVE
MEDAL

TO GARRETT A. MORGAN
INVENTOR OF MORGAN
NAT. SAFETY HOOD
A LIFE SAVING DEVICE

Garrett won first prize at a national safety exposition.

He received a United States patent in 1914 for his invention.

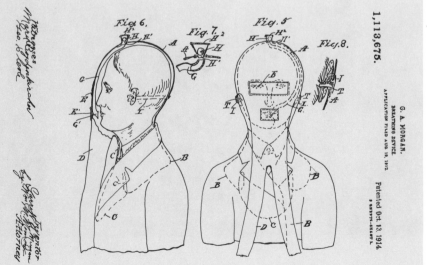

45

Many people were hurt. Garrett invented an electric light signal. The different-colored lights told the driver when to go or stop. That was the beginning of the traffic-light system we still use today.

After Garrett patented his traffic signal, he sold the rights to the General Electric Corporation for $40,000.00.

Garrett cared very deeply about his fellow black Americans. He felt that the newspapers in Cleveland didn't give fair

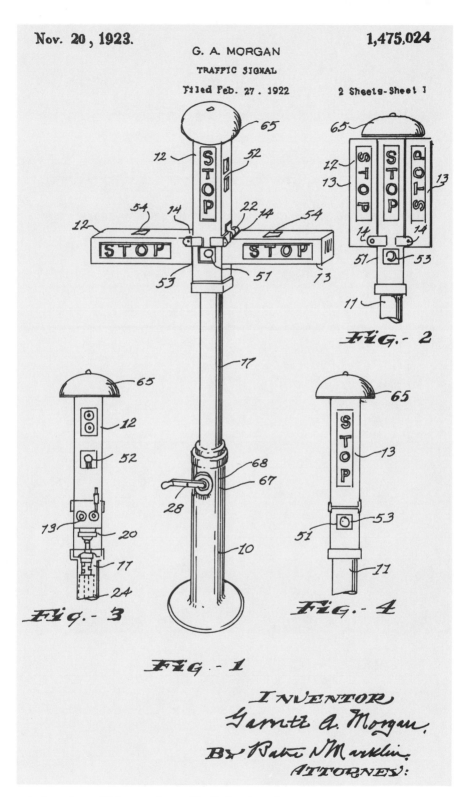

G. A. MORGAN

TRAFFIC SIGNAL

Filed Feb. 27, 1922

2 Sheets-Sheet 1

Fig.- 2

Fig.- 3

Fig.- 4

Fig.- 1

INVENTOR

Garrett A. Morgan,

By Baker N Marklin.

ATTORNEY:

A drawing of Morgan's traffic light signal.

attention to events in the black community. So he founded the *Cleveland Call* newspaper. It is now called the *Cleveland Call & Post*. Then in 1931, Garrett ran for the city council in Cleveland. He wanted to give black people better representation in city government.

Garrett Morgan lived a long and successful life. He was 86 years old when he died.